Chester Chipmunk's Thanksgiving

by BARBARA WILLIAMS

illustrated by KAY CHORAO

E. P. Dutton   New York

Library of Congress Cataloging in Publication Data

Williams, Barbara.   Chester Chipmunk's Thanksgiving.

SUMMARY: Chester Chipmunk can't seem to find anybody
to share his Thanksgiving dinner.
[1. Thanksgiving Day—Fiction]   I. Chorao, Kay.   II. Title.
PZ7.W65587Ch   [E]   77-20812   ISBN: 0-525-27655-6

Published in the United States by E. P. Dutton, a Division
of Sequoia-Elsevier Publishing Company, Inc., New York
Published simultaneously in Canada by Clarke,
Irwin & Company Limited, Toronto and Vancouver

Editor: Ann Durell   Designer: Meri Shardin
Printed in the U.S.A.
10 9 8 7 6 5 4 3 2

To Ann Durell
and all the other members
of the W.E.F.A.D.S.P.

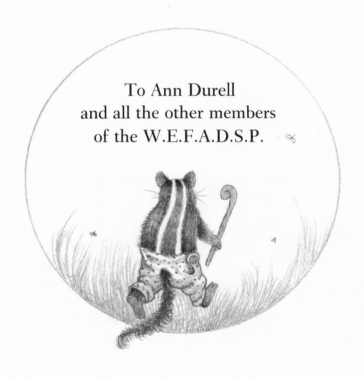

On Thanksgiving Day, Chester Chipmunk had many things to be grateful for. He enjoyed good health. He had a nice big burrow to live in. He had a nice new cloak and walking stick. And he had collected more than enough pecans to last him through the winter.

But as Chester looked at all his piles of nuts, he felt a little sad. His cousin Archie lived in a tiny, cramped burrow, and he was always too sick from lumbago or high blood pressure or fallen arches to go nut collecting. Poor Archie was probably sitting in his uncomfortable house right now, wondering what he was going to eat for Thanksgiving dinner.

Chester jumped up suddenly and started to sing as he put some eggs, sugar, and corn syrup in a bowl to make a pecan pie. When the pie was baked, he set it to cool and scampered over to Cousin Archie's burrow.

"Yoohoo, Cousin Archie!" called Chester. "YOOHOO!"

"Goodness, Chester," said Cousin Archie. "What are you doing outside in weather like this? You'll catch your death of pneumonia."

"It isn't very cold, Cousin Archie," Chester explained. "Anyway, I had to come over to invite you to dinner. I baked a nice pecan pie for Thanksgiving, and I don't want to eat it by myself. Thanksgiving is a day you should share with your relatives."

"Heavens, Chester, you know my lumbago acts up when I go outside in weather like this," said Cousin Archie. "You just go home and enjoy your nice pecan pie by yourself and think of me sitting here cold and hungry." And he shut the door.

Chester started sadly toward home, but when he was halfway there, he heard a voice from overhead.

"Hi there, Chester," called Oswald Opossum, who was hanging by his tail from a tree. "You shouldn't be out gathering nuts today. Don't you know it's a holiday? Don't you know it's Thanksgiving?"

"I'm not gathering nuts, Oswald. I'm just—"

"You don't need to tell me what you're doing, Chester. Don't I see everything that goes on in these woods from my branch in this tree?"

"I suppose, but—"

"Well then, you go home right now and bake a nice Thanksgiving pie with some of those pecans you've gathered."

Chester didn't bother to answer. He just trotted back to his burrow and stared at his pecan pie. After a while he heard the Woodchuck twins outside playing ball. That gave Chester an idea, and he jumped up suddenly and started to sing as he put some eggs, sugar, and corn syrup in a bowl to make another pecan pie. When the pie was baked, he set it to cool and scurried over to Mrs. Woodchuck's burrow.

"Yoohoo, Mrs. Woodchuck!" called Chester.
"YOOHOO!"

"Is that you, Chester?" she called back. "I can't
come to the door right now. I'm in the middle of
making some crabgrass stew for Thanksgiving
dinner."

"That's all right, Mrs. Woodchuck," answered
Chester. "I just came over to invite you and the
twins to share the two nice pecan pies I baked for
Thanksgiving dinner. Why don't you bring your
crabgrass stew along, and we can all eat together."

"That's very nice of you, Chester," said Mrs. Woodchuck, "but my aunt and uncle from Natchez will be here at any minute. We always eat dinner with our relatives on Thanksgiving."

"Well, maybe another time," said Chester sadly. Then suddenly Chester had an idea, and he darted home to his burrow to get his new cloak.

"Yoohoo, Cousin Archie!" Chester called outside Archie's burrow. "YOOHOO!"

"Goodness, Chester," said Archie. "What are you doing here again?"

"Look, Cousin Archie. I brought you my nice warm cloak so you can walk to my burrow for Thanksgiving dinner. I baked two pecan pies, and I don't want to eat them by myself. Thanksgiving is a day you should share with your relatives."

"Heavens, Chester, you know I can't walk all the way to your burrow with my fallen arches," said Cousin Archie. "You just go home and enjoy your two nice pecan pies by yourself and think of me sitting here unable to walk, alone and hungry." And he shut the door.

Chester headed toward home, but when he was halfway there, he heard Oswald Opossum calling from his branch in the tree.

"Are you still gathering nuts?" asked Oswald.

"I'm not gathering nuts, Oswald. I'm just—"

"Can't I see you with my own eyes? Don't I know who gathers nuts in this forest and who doesn't?" asked Oswald.

"I suppose, but—"

"Well then, it's time you stopped gathering nuts and invited someone to Thanksgiving dinner. Don't you know that some people don't have any nuts so that they can bake their own pecan pies?"

Chester didn't bother to answer. He just went
on home and stared at his two pecan pies, which
he didn't feel at all like eating. After a while he
heard the Cottontail children outside playing tag.

That gave Chester an idea, and he jumped up suddenly and started to sing as he put some eggs, sugar, and corn syrup in a bowl to make three more pecan pies. When the pies were baked, he set them to cool and skittered over to Mrs. Cottontail's nest.

"Yoohoo, Mrs. Cottontail!" called Chester. "YOOHOO!"

"Come in, Chester, and help Brunhilda and me stir all this carrot pudding," answered Mrs. Cottontail. "I'm trying to cook Thanksgiving dinner, and I'm so nervous I'm all paws."

"Why don't you relax and bring your children over to my house for dinner?" asked Chester. "I baked five pecan pies for Thanksgiving, and I don't have anyone to share them with."

"That's very nice of you, Chester," said Mrs. Cottontail, "but my sister Geraldine and her five children are coming to dinner at my house."

"No, Mama," said Brunhilda. "Aunt Geraldine has six children. But you didn't invite her. You invited Aunt Stella and her seven children."

"Dear me!" exclaimed Mrs. Cottontail. "You mean your Aunt Geraldine and her six children are going hungry on Thanksgiving? You rush right over to her nest and invite her to dinner, Brunhilda, while I peel some more carrots." She turned to Chester. "Thank you for your invitation, but we always eat dinner with our relatives on Thanksgiving."

"Well, maybe another time," said Chester sadly. Then suddenly Chester had an idea, and he sprinted home to his burrow to get his new walking stick.

"Yoohoo, Cousin Archie!" Chester called outside Archie's burrow. "YOOHOO!"

"Goodness, Chester," said Cousin Archie. "You woke me up from my nap."

"I'm sorry, Archie," said Chester, "but I'm hoping you've changed your mind about coming to my burrow for dinner. I brought you my walking stick to lean on so your fallen arches won't bother you. I baked five nice pecan pies for Thanksgiving dinner, and I don't want to eat them by myself. Thanksgiving is a day you should share with your relatives."

"Heavens, Chester, you know I have to take a nap every afternoon for my high blood pressure," said Cousin Archie. "You just go home and enjoy your five nice pecan pies by yourself and think of me lying here alone and hungry." And he shut the door.

Chester started wearily toward home. Then he had another idea. "Yoohoo, Oswald Opossum!" he called. "YOOHOO!"

"You don't have to shout at me, Chester," said Oswald. "Don't you know I'm not deaf?"

"Oswald, I took your advice and baked five pecan pies for Thanksgiving dinner. Will you please come to my house and share them with me?"

"Well, I thought you'd never ask!" said Oswald. "I don't mind if I do." And he unwound his tail from his branch and flipped to the ground.

The friends were just cutting the first piece of pecan pie when they heard voices outside Chester's burrow.

"Yoohoo, Chester!" called Mrs. Woodchuck. "YOOHOO! I told my aunt and uncle from Natchez about your two pecan pies, and they suggested we bring over this crabgrass stew and eat Thanksgiving dinner together."

"Yoohoo, Chester," called Mrs. Cottontail. "YOOHOO! I told my sisters and their children about your five pecan pies, and they all suggested we bring over this carrot pudding and eat Thanksgiving dinner together."

"Yoohoo, Cousin Chester!" called Cousin
Archie. "YOOHOO! What are all these strangers
doing here? Don't they know Thanksgiving is a
day you share with relatives?"

"Don't you know a friend is someone who lets you have the pleasure of giving?" asked Oswald Opossum.

"Don't you know all this food is waiting to be eaten?" said Chester Chipmunk.

BARBARA WILLIAMS says that Chester Chipmunk's experience is her own—every year. "About November 1, my husband and I start inviting his college students to Thanksgiving dinner. Ninety-five percent have other plans. The other five percent say 'Maybe.' Then on Thanksgiving Day, the Nos begin knocking on the door, bringing along extra friends. We love having them, but I wish *just once* I could set the correct number of places at the table beforehand!"

KAY CHORAO found the theme of giving and sharing the most appealing aspect of Chester Chipmunk's story. "From my experience with children, generosity is an attribute which must be learned. And so this book offers a happy and appropriate message for the young—giving the Thanksgiving holiday more significance." This is the fourth book on which the author and illustrator have collaborated.

The title is Goudy Handtooled set in typositor. The other display and text are Fairfield Medium set in Fototronic Savant. The art was drawn with pencil. The book was printed by offset at Halliday Lithographers.

H13252